WILLY WHYNER, CLOUD DESIGNER

by
Michael and Esther Lustig

Four Winds Press ⋚ᴹ⋚ New York

Maxwell Macmillan Canada   Toronto
Maxwell Macmillan International
New York

Willy Whyner's parents were very serious people. They wore serious clothes and had very serious jobs.

They were not at all happy with Willy Whyner. He spent too much time dreaming and playing games and building totally useless things.

One day Willy Whyner asked his father, Wilber Whyner, why clouds always stuck together in great big fluffy clumps.

Wilber Whyner was a man who knew many complicated and useful things. He even knew how to comb his hair in a special way to hide the big bald spot in the middle of his head. He didn't waste his time with silly questions. "Stop wasting my time and go do your homework," said Wilber Whyner.

Willy's mother, Wanda Whyner, was a very clever woman. For thirty years she had been smart enough to say nothing about the strange way that Wilber Whyner combed his hair.
Willy asked her about the clouds. "Stop worrying about clouds and finish eating," said Wanda Whyner.

Willy finished eating, but he couldn't stop wondering about clouds. He read every book he could find about clouds or wind or weather. He wouldn't talk about baseball or rocket ships or dinosaurs or vampires or ghosts . . . only clouds.

Nobody paid much attention to Why Whyler and his clouds until the night that everybody's electricity suddenly blew out.

It was dark and quiet everywhere,
except for Willy's room, which exploded
with color and light. The wind howled and
lightning crackled. An angry crowd
soon gathered at Willy's house
to find out what was
happening.

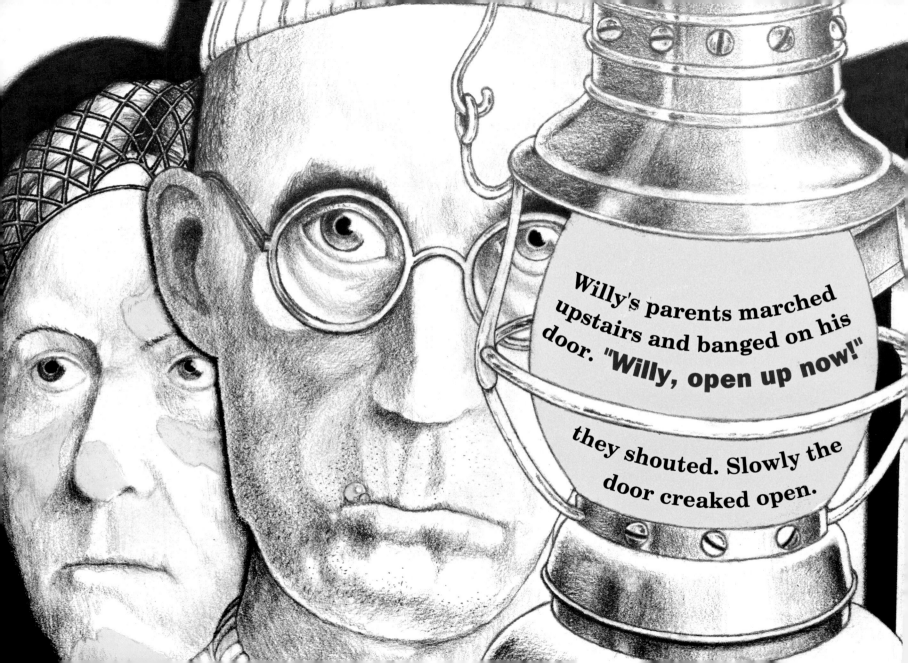

Willy was in the corner with smoke coming out of his hair. On the table was a broken humidifier that Willy's father had once gotten for only 99 cents at a garage sale. Blinking and whizzing around it was a whole bunch of stuff that had been missing for months. Inside the humidifier was a perfectly wonderful little cloud.

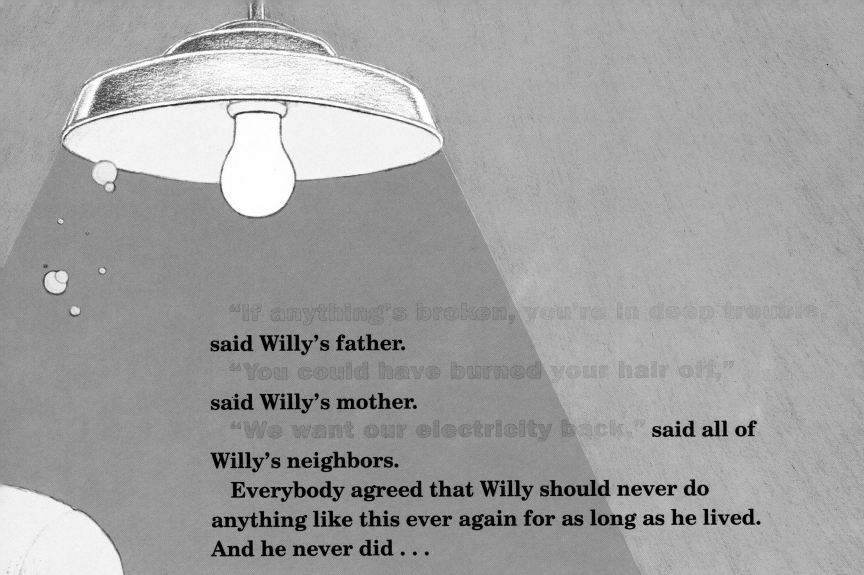

"If anything's broken, you're in deep trouble,"
said Willy's father.
"You could have burned your hair off,"
said Willy's mother.
"We want our electricity back," said all of
Willy's neighbors.
  Everybody agreed that Willy should never do
anything like this ever again for as long as he lived.
And he never did . . .

. . . until he went into business as Willy Whyner, Cloud Designer, Incorporated, and held a meeting in his kitchen with a gang of international bankers.

Soon mysterious-looking factories began opening up all over the world and people everywhere started seeing some very unusual-looking clouds.

The newspapers were filled with amazing stories about clouds. One newspaper said it had proof that the clouds came to Earth from the planet Mars. Everyone wondered what would happen next. They soon found out.

The world's first experimental advertising cloud appeared over the town of Buzzard Creek, Idaho, and was an astonishing success. Edna's Tiptop Luncheonette had so many customers that Willy's aunt Edna opened more luncheonettes in nearby Buzzardburg, Buzzard's Gulch, and the Buzzard Falls Mall.

Suddenly every business had to have its own advertising clouds, no matter how much they cost. People started bringing Willy truckloads of cash and toys in the middle of the night, hoping to get moved up on his waiting list.

When the authorities found
out that Willy wasn't a grown-up,
he had to sell his business for $14 billion
and go back to finish the third grade. That
ended the story of Willy Whyner, Cloud Designer,
but it wasn't quite the end of the story of the clouds.
Before long, the sky was so full of unusual clouds that
you couldn't see the Sun or the Moon or the stars.